THE MINER STORIES BOOK THREE

FIRESTONES:
The MINER
BOOK THREE

S.E. McKenzie

ISBN-10: 1772810290

DEDICATION
To the miners everywhere who should have been safer.

This book is a book of Fiction.

Characters, companies, governments, places, events, are either products of the author's imagination or used fictitiously. Any resemblance to persons (living or dead), companies, governments, places and/or events, is a coincidence.

CONTENTS

"

"

Chapter 1
The Aftermath

December 31st 2030, around 10:00 PM: " What a horrible New Year's Eve. This whole Christmas has been the worst one in my entire life. Everyone is either dead or almost dead. I am stuck here on a boat in the middle of the Arctic Ocean. It is dark and cold and there is a continual cracking and humming noise," Mathew said.

"Mathew, don't be so glum. Alright as an artist there may be a good argument for feeling glum, but as scientists we must stay objective. Science is a wonderful thing. Science keeps your mother alive; science keeps your brother is alive. And as you can see baby James is growing like a weed. You are much better off here anyway. There are too troubles in Pitville,' James explained.

"I wanted to go to Ginger's funeral but my mom and my little brother might die next so that is why I am here. Everyone seems to go so fast without any goodbye. It is almost like a domino effect first Ginger gets shot and then Jay, George Kevin and Sam just disappear," Mathew Watson Junior said.

"I have been to enough funerals in my day to know how funerals wind people up to tears. Funerals can bring back the diseased and wind people up beyond the comfort zone," James said.

"My grandmother says that funerals are meant to remember and share those life memories of the person who just died," Mathew interjected.

"I can just imagine your grandmother saying that. Though you call me Uncle James, and there is nothing wrong with that, I am really your new step dad, and we are going to have a new beginning here. We are going to see a new world, a new way of life. And to top it off we will be observing how Minese and associates thrive while living under a ten day calendar and a ten hour clock," James explained.

"A ten day calendar? How does that work?"

"It is very complicated. The calculations at the moment are top secret. The folks in Mina have been operating under this revolutionary calendar for some time and it seems to be working for them, so I am sure it will work for Coalton Valley 2. As for Jay, George, Kevin and Sam, I am sure that they are lost on purpose, probably avoiding their wives' scorn for drinking too much on Christmas Eve. And poor Ginger, I feel terrible that he is gone. This horrible year will be over in two hours. Your mother and baby James..." James Coaltonstone said before he was interrupted.

"How can anyone be lost for a week and why do you keep calling him Baby James instead of baby Ginger?

"Most people who go missing are running away from something and Ginger is not a name, it is a nick name. James is a fine name and suits your baby brother to a T. James is a name which commands..."

"What happens if people get his name mixed up with yours and he gets shot when he grows up?"

"Why would anyone want to shoot me? Anyway, I have expanded my body guard crew to include ten of the state of the art guard bots. Where people have failed me my bots will make up for it. I am sure when the time come when needed these bots will surpass all my expectations," James said expecting Mathew not to reply.

"At least your bots don't die. I don't know why it feels like people want to kill you. It just does. Everyone blames you for Ginger's death. But I don't. Who is to blame for Ginger's death, Uncle James?" Mathew said.

"Sometimes there isn't anyone to blame though John Bell is blaming Ginger and says that he shot him in self-defense," James replied.

"Ginger would never hurt anyone even those people who seem to be almost stepping on him all the time," Mathew said louder than he normally spoke.

"This entire week has been unbelievably terrible. Ginger was so young and his whole life is gone. Don's wife is scheduled for surgery on Friday and I won't be there. Christina is getting stronger but she doesn't seem to want to wake up. I have never had a patient as small as this baby but he seems to be making up for his size by being brave." Ashley said without meaning to interrupt.

"Well he is a Coaltonstone, of course he is brave. It has always been the Coaltonstone way.

"I miss Ginger. I miss my mother nd I wish that my brother was a lot bigger. I wish I knew what really happened to Ginger." Mathew said.

"Sometimes we never find out what really happens but over time there will never be a shortage of opinions. We just have to remember all the people who benefitted from Ginger's life and quick thinking right before the explosion in Mine Five. It would be nice if they named the Parkway after him. That would be one way of honoring him for being such a friend. That reminds me, I have your birthday present right here in my right pocket. And your Christmas present in my left. Is it okay if Mathew opens them now Dr. Knight?

"Certainly," Ashley replied.

"Thank you very much Uncle James," Mathew said as he opened up the box. "You gave me a gun for my birthday? Is it real?" Mathew asked.

"It certainly is. And what do I have in my left pocket? Your belated Christmas present which is a pocket full of ammunition. What do you think about that?"

"Did you get baby Ginger a gun too, Uncle James?"

"Not yet. I did get him his fancy life support system which is doing a very good job keeping him alive, with the help of Doctor Knight's gifted hands, may I add."

"I am trying my best Mr. Coaltonstone, but I can't perform miracles?" Ashley replied.

"You certainly can," James interjected.

"So until baby Ginger gets his own gun, how will people not get your name mixed up with his? You are always in the newspaper and baby Ginger looks so innocent and tiny. He sort of looks like an alien," Mathew said.

"First of all, baby James' last name is hyphenated just like your new name is. So you both are going to have Watson-Coaltonstone as a last name, now. A double barrel name if I have ever heard one," James said as he grabbed another bottle of water from the fridge. Anyone need anything to drink?

"Sure I will have a water. Is that your face on the water bottle Uncle James?

"It sure is. It is my label that goes on all of my products," James explained.

"Why doesn't baby Ginger have Goodwin as part of his name?" Mathew asked.

"Because the baby's name has been legally changed but like yours has been. Like I said before you are both Coaltonstones. And I have a feeling you both will be great ones. Your little brother has already defied the odds. He lives, he breathes, and one day he will join the chapter of our special club which is just open to men," James predicted.

"Why don't you let women join?" Mathew asked. "I don't know if I would want to belong to a club that women were not allowed to join."

"It is tradition. We are a man's club. You will soon learn how distracting women can be," James said.

"If the truth be known Mathew, most men are terrified of women," Ashley interjected.

"And with good reason," James said as he sipped his water.

"Are you sure you and baby James won't get shot one day the way Ginger was?" Mathew asked.

"Absolutely sure, all true enemies usually want each other to stay alive. A man in my position may wonder who his friends are, but true enemies give meaning to life and can be blamed for all kinds of things," James said.

"So what do you think happened to Jay, George, Kevin and Sam? Do you think Mr. Bell shot them the way he shot Ginger?" Mathew asked.

"We have no idea what happened to them but my guess is they are hiding from their wives. What happened to Ginger was most a terrible and tragic accident," James Coaltonstone replied.

"What actually happened to Ginger?"

"I don't know yet," James replied.

"Is that true Doctor Knight or is Uncle James lying to me?"

"I am sure Mr. Coaltonstone is saying the truth his way, just like he always does," Ashley said.

"Okay, I will tell you something but it is a secret as in 'inside information', so you must swear that you won't give our secret away to anyone," James explained. "And that means you too, Ashley," James said as he winked.

"You have my word, Uncle James."

"You know everything you say to me in confidence stays here," Ashley replied.

"Okay, the secret is, I belong to a lodge and…"

"Is that the secret?" Mathew asked.

"Yes, partly, we have members all over the world, which means that many of our members are citizens of countries which are in conflict with each other. But brothers don't kill brothers. We have secret handshakes, secret words, secret agendas, and one day Mathew you will be invited to join."

"Why?"

"Because you have what it takes to be a brother of our order. You made $10,000 selling your photos, you have modified your flyke suit so you were able to flyke all the way here to visit us and your new brother. You are staying on our state of the heart ice melting ship. In life, son, what nature does can be devastating, but the power of money and brother can make up for some of it. Not all of it son, but some," James Coaltonstone said.

Mathew continued to look glum. "Uncle James, that gun and those bullets give me a very eerie feeling. Can we put them away?"

"Certainly, I thought it would be fun, to have a little target practice first thing we do at the beginning of the New Year," James suggested.

"How can we see the target, it is dark here all the time, all you can see are things that are lit up like drones and other people on boats," Mathew said.

"Ships, Mathew ships. We are on a ship not a rowboat. Did you notice all the drones flying back and forth? James asked.

"I did, they almost flew into me even though I am lit up just as much as a Christmas tree as all the other flykers," Mathew said.

"So where do you think all those drones are going and what do you think they are carrying?" James asked fighting back a smile which made Ashley smile for this was a side of the King of Coal very few would ever see.

"I bet they are carrying all kinds of Christmas presents," Mathew said.

"I think so too. Those drones are probably carrying all kinds of presents. Presents that were late being shipped, presents that were sent to the wrong address and now have to be returned to be resent. I bet there are all kinds of presents that fell through the cracks of the system, and if we shoot them down, they didn't only fall through the cracks in the system, they will be falling out of the sky into our laps. Even the unwanted presents could fall right into our laps," James replied.

"You think we should shoot down drones, Uncle James?" Mathew asked. "I saw protestors do that but I don't feel right doing that even if they were taking my picture. I think the drones were taking photos of the protestors before the protestors shot them down.

"I am sure your Uncle James would never do that, he is kidding, right Mr. Coaltonstone," Ashley asked James.

"I certainly am not. But if the boy does not feel right shooting down drones, he is a much better man than I," James said as he winked at Mathew.

"Seriously now, if we put your gun and ammo away we must them where we can get hold of them quickly if we have to. We might need your gun and my gun if those riff raff you saw on the way here board our ship without being granted permission," James said as he padded his coat pocket.

"You are kidding again, right, Uncle James?"

"I certainly am not. I follow the law of the sea. If it were up to me I would be following the French Revolutionary Calendar and today would not be New Year's Eve and I would only have to pay my workers for one day of rest every ten days instead of seven." James explained.

"You are joking right. How could anyone work for 10 days without rest. I need to rest on Sunday, at least. I sure miss everyone. I wish they were here. Or maybe I wish that I were with them right now," Mathew said.

"Mathew, you are doing very well, and don't feel guilty for doing so well when others around you are suffering. Sometimes that is one of the hardest things to learn how to do, isn't that right Mr. Coaltonstone."

"Well, that never bothered…"

"Mr. Coaltonstone!" Ashley exclaimed horrified that her humanist approach to life could be hijacked by James Coaltonstone's Machiavellian tendencies.

"My mother might be close to death and the only reason why my brother is alive is because Uncle James forced the hospital to sell him one of their incubators. It is cold and dark here all day long. And once we cross the Bering Strait we will have entered the military zone and everyone will be cross. You know Uncle James, I am hungry, can we eat now?"

"Having our last meal of the year together is grand idea, isn't that right Dr. Knight?"

"Certainly, I am getting hungry myself and I am sure Dr. Smith is even hungrier than I am.

"You see, Mathew. The world is not the happiest of places unless we make it happy. And little James is growing every minute. He is a little fighter. Your mother had an accident but she is going to recover nicely, isn't she Doctor Knight?" Coaltonstone gave Ashley such an intense glare it scared her.

"I am doing my best. That is all we can ever do," Ashley replied.

"No, as long as we best our competitors we win, regardless if it is our best or not," James said with a slight grin on his face. Ashley's make shift office on James' ship was adequate but not comfortable and James was beginning to feel cramping in his long legs..

"Now, Mathew, you have to be a little bit more positive or you will drive yourself insane and I would have failed you as your physician," Ashley added.

"So tell me what is good about my life right now."

"First of all you will be witnessing history. We are building a very new town beside Cold Feet Mountain," James said.

"The protestors have signs saying that you are moving a cemetery and a bunch of dead people to make room for Coalton Valley 2, that you bought the land super cheap and it could even be radioactive. Is that true?"

"Would the protestors prefer that I build our new town right on top of the cemetery?"

"Mr. Coaltonstone!"

"There are lots of things to be thankful for," James Coaltonstone said as he winked at Ashley. "You will be seeing the other side of Bering Strait which is a great privilege. And most important of all, you are now a Coaltonstone; a hyphenated one, but still a Coaltonstone. Your mother is in good hands and is recovering day by day. Isn't that right Doctor Knight?"

"We are doing the best we can sir under the circumstances," Ashley replied.

"I am sure you are. And Doctor Smith is attending to your mother and your little brother as we speak. You have money in the bank that is earning interest. The New Year will be rocky and at the same time very exciting. Just keep moving forward young man," James said.

"Mathew, your Mother needs to see a brave face when she wakes up and she will need to see a smiling face," Ashley said as she patted Mathew's knee.

"Quite right and you will love my castle. All the houses that can be moved from Pitville to Coalton Valley 2 are being moved. So once Coalton Valley 2 is set up, it will remind you of your old home in Pitville. It will just take time to adjust to everything, but Pitville is not what it used to be. That is what happens in life, things change, often for the bad. Only the winners thrive under such circumstance and only one person can win the race.

"What will the people left behind in Pitville do, Uncle James?"

"This will be a very exciting time for the tourist industry. We are arranging tours of the mines including Ginger's escape route, complete with ladders, ropes and special effects."

"What about all the protests? What about the coal seam fire? Have they been able to put it out yet?" Mathew asked.

"No, the coal seam fire is still burning. I am sure it will add to the value of the Pitville economy though. The tourists will soon be flocking to the smoke coming out of the roads and sidewalks," James replied.

"What about the polar bear protestors?" Mathew asked.

"You mean the polar bears are protesting too?"

"Uncle James, you know what I mean. Protestors are out on boats trying to save the polar bears."

"And those protestors know polar bears are meat eaters, right? Anyway, if the bears don't take care of them, I will have John Bell handle them in the same way we handle all of them."

"Isn't he the guy who killed Ginger? I hate him."

"Now, Mathew," Ashley interjected.

"I am sorry, Doctor Knight I just do hate him."

"Well we don't know what happened," James said wishing that he hadn't mentioned John Bell's name, and made a mental note to never mention his name to Mathew again."

"So, is Mr. Bell going to kill the protestors the way he killed Ginger?"

"Mathew, what happened to Ginger was a mistake. And if the protestors don't attack us, we won't have any reason to shoot them. That is the law of the sea," James said.

"What about the ones on the ship I saw when I flyked in? They seemed to be really concerned for the Polar Bears that have been found drowning or cannibalizing each other," Mathew said.

"Well those people need someone to hit them over the head."

"Mr. Coaltonstone, I do not think such comments are very helpful." Ashley intervened.

"Dr. Ashley, why am I being blamed for polar bear cannibalism? Next thing you know I will be blamed for poor Doctor Max's sudden heart attack that he suffered while on vacation, before he was scheduled to speak on how human behavior is effecting climate change," James complained.

"I think the issue here is that the polar bears' ice habitat is melting, which changes how these bears are able to follow their instincts. Bears are drowning, and bears are resorting to each other to ward off hunger."

"And you think we humans would not resort to cannibalism if we could not expand ways to grow food for themselves. If those protestors are so concerned for the polar bears' health why don't they just jump in the ocean and make the world a better place."

"Mr. Coaltonstone, really. This family meeting is losing its focus to say the least," Ashley said.

"Well those protestors are ruining everything. They are interfering with my way of life and encouraging my miners to strike."

"A lot has ruined my life too. My mom is on life support, my brother is on life support, Ginger is dead. Why did Mr. Bell kill Ginger, Uncle James?" Mathew asked.

"We don't know yet. John said Ginger had a gun," James replied.

"Ginger hated guns, he would have been a conscientious objector if they had allowed him to do that," Doctor Smith said as he rushed into the meeting room to defend Ginger's honor. "Where did you come from, Dan?" James Coaltonstone asked.

"I was stretching my legs and couldn't help but over hear your family meeting. I am sorry, James. I guess I got carried away. I delivered Ginger as you know.

"You did?" Mathew asked. "Wow. Was he has small as baby Ginger."

"You mean baby James," James interjected as Ashley threw her hands up in the air in exasperation."

"No Mathew, your baby brother is a preemie and our friend Ginger was full term." Doctor Smith explained.

"Oh," Mathew replied as he looked at Doctor Smith's watch.

"I can't bring Ginger back, but we can celebrate his life while introducing some of my new products. We will be serving Coaltonstone beef and Coaltonstone beer. We will be selling all kinds of souvenirs. Your baby brother will grow, and whatever weakness he has, he will find the strength inside himself to meet the challenge. And you, young man are a very talented photographer; you have sold your photographs. You must have a very handsome account balance as we speak."

"Actually I have around seven thousand and nine-hundred and fifty-seven dollars left. I took rest stops at a couple of Starbucks and MacDonald's in between here and Pitville. I also added some new features to my suit before I left. I had to get a really good head lamp and a down suit. It is so dark and cold all the time here.

"You have a great flyking suit. It is amazing that you flyked all the way here."

"If birds can do it, why can't I?"

"No reason at all. That is exactly what I mean. Bad things happen and good things happen. The work we will be doing up in the Arctic will make that part of the world more habitable to humans and easier to mine. During this decade we will own the weather, Mathew. Bad things will always happen in this world. And we have to find ways to survive and stick it out no matter what. Owning the weather is part of that struggle. The future will is full of promise. The Arctic owns more than a fifth of the world's oil and gas resources, rare earth metals, coal, uranium, gold, diamonds, zinc, platinum; mostly untapped and there for the taking. All we have to do is quicken the melting of the ice caps, tilt Earth's axis a little, and we could turn the Arctic into a warmer and more habitable where the wealth becomes accessible."

"How are you going to do that, Uncle James?"

"We are hoping that our private submarines blasting the ice with nuclear warhead will work otherwise we will have to wait until one of the many countries at war decide to throw nuclear bombs at each other, which could be any day now," James said

"How are we going to survive a nuclear war," Mathew asked.

"We will have to keep our distance son and work on peaceful uses so that one day we can own and control the weather now. Just imagine the world with an ice free Arctic Ocean would mean a huge boom in oceanic shipping between Europe and East Asia. The wastelands in Northern Canada and Siberia would be free for farming, increasing the food production supply for all. An ice Free Arctic would lead to more rain even in desert regions. Imagine the world with more places to grow food. Many people, including myself believe that the prophecy in the bible, turning weapons into ploughshares, meant this type of project. Where we can use nuclear energy for good, and expand shipping roots, free up more farmland while expanding our mining capacity."

"But Uncle James wouldn't melting the ice caps lead to more global warming, tilting of Earth's axis toward Canada and raise sea levels? What about all that radiation. Isn't that why there are so many protestors following us, because they claim that people you know were hiding radioactive materials, and those materials led to people getting cancer who wouldn't have normally gotten it. And how did people in the old days, when the bible was written, know about nuclear energy and nuclear weapons?"

"Just imagine a warmer world, Mathew? Imagine a world without hunger."

"But Uncle James what will happen when the see level rises."

"It won't rise that much. This coming New Year will be grand. I promise."

"But Uncle James what happens if the Arctic Ice comes back."

"It won't."

"How do you know? Weather seems to be getting harder to predict."

"Because this year I am going to own the weather. Don't look so surprised. Think of all the coal I own. It is just logical that I should own the weather too. Besides that, ice will be harder to form when the sun's radiation no longer has ice to reflect upon sending it back into the Arctic Sky. Once the ice is gone, the sun's radiation won't be able to reflect back into the sky the way it does now, so the retained heat will keep the Arctic ice from coming back ," James said.

"And what about the rest of the world?" Mathew asked.

"What about it?" James replied.

"People say that that when the Polar Ice Caps melt, the earth could change its tilt, seasons could be effected, and oceans could rise and drown all kinds of people all over the world," Mathew said.

"The brothers that belong to our lodge will be fine. They are builders and problem solvers and most of them are very good swimmers, may I add."

"What about everyone else?" Mathew asked.

"What about them?" James asked back.

Chapter 2
Waiting for Alex

December 31st 2030, around 10:00 PM: "Where is Alex Coaltonstone? I thought our main focus at this meeting was to focus costs related to moving Coalton Valley, or as much as we can of it, to our new location. I bet you anything he has been delayed by all those protestors taking over the streets."

"Actually sir, they are going to a memorial meeting for Ginger Goodwin. Since the autopsy has delayed the funeral, the public needed to celebrate his life and his death and his senseless shooting," Susan said as she her eyes fixed on her computer screen. "I could phone him, sir," Susan Jones offered.

"Why, haven't you already?"

"I was taking notes, sir," Susan replied beginning to sound as nervous as she felt.

"As you know James is speculating in the Arctic…"

"I thought he was looking for Polar Ice Caps to Nuke," Susan interrupted.

Mayor Stern looked at Susan sternly and continued. "Nevertheless, James has assured me that Alex would be costing the moving to Coalton Valley 2 operation, in real time not his time."

"Excuse me, I think the coffee is here, Susan please get the door," Mayor Stone ordered nicely. As Susan opened the door a drone flew in carrying four cups of from in broad daylight at Starbucks I have been using this service and I love it. As you can see I ordered Alex a cup of latté in its cargo container.

"Ever since my car was stolen I wish I had used this service before my car had been stolen," Mayor Stern said.

"Didn't you get your car back Mr. Stern? I thought I saw it parked in the driveway," Susan said.

"Yes, I got the car back but the schedule with very special calculations, which James had been sourced out, is missing and James is furious with me. Why we had no other copies made is beyond me," Mayor Stern said not even trying to hide the exasperation he was feeling. This was New Year's Eve. His wife was hosting a small get together with Club Leaders.

"Why would a schedule be top secret?" Susan asked.

"Beats me," Mayor Stern replied.

"Sir, shouldn't we also be costing security in Pitville? Jethro and Bill have sent urgent email to John that those protestors hanging out on Cold Feet Mountain are just as furious as the protestors are who are hanging out in Pitville. They are upset that Ginger was shot, upset that the Mine doesn't seem to be opening so men are now out of work. They are upset that the loans James will be granting to unemployed miners will have a 10% interest rate which will be compounding semi-annually attached to them. Now there is intelligence that the schedule that Mr. Stern is talking about is the protestors' hands, and there are thousands of copies being made," Don explained.

"I don't get it, with all that is going on, why would anyone care about a schedule?" Susan asked.

"I don't know but Jethro and Bill are assuming that all this anger will lead to violence. Today's protest has been going on all day and into the night. The situation is very dangerous. You don't need to be an intelligence officer to figure that out," Don said.

"Funeral, Don, it is a funeral. I don't understand. What is the big deal about the schedule?" Susan interjected.

"How can we cost something what we don't know is going to happen? These protestors, as a class of human being, are impossible to predict. We need to talk about the costs related to the moving of our most valuable structures to the Coalton Valley 2 location. Our new location in the cave country is beautiful and will be great, and we need Alex here so can be briefed on costs," Mayor Stern said.

"How are the locals handling the moving of their cemetery?" Susan asked.

"Pretty much as expected; we have air surveillance overseeing operations. Those assets are working beyond our most optimistic expectations. The whistle bots call shift cycles and the deportees are obeying those signals, as if their lives depend on them following the ten day week as if they were still in Mina." Mayor Stern said.

"For how long?" Don asked.

"For as long as they live, and they better obey all orders for as long as we say, if they want their lives to be long," Mayor Stern said.

"You are kidding right?" Susan asked.

"What do you think, Susan? Choosing that flat spot near Cold Feet Mountain as our new base was a stroke of brilliance. The mountain is already proving to be very profitable and is more than making up for the wasteful work stoppage these protestors are causing," Mayor Stern said as he slammed his coffee cup down on his huge Brazilian mahogany desk, unintentionally. "The disruptions to our way of life by these outsiders, is unacceptable. Our most capable deportees are being sent as replacements and will be bunked under Coalton Valley 2," Mayor Stern explained.

"Sir, the work stoppage is in honor of Ginger Goodwin. Everyone has all kinds of emotions. Some are still in shock and still can't believe that Ginger of all people is dead. Others are furious that John shot him and don't believe it was necessary," Susan said as she was still waiting for Alex to answer his phone.

"I just hope that those protestors don't mistake me for him," Don said trying to not sound like he was whining.

"Just keep wearing your name tag," Susan said as she covered the mouth piece of her phone with her hand.

"Where is Alex? Why can't you get him on the phone?" Mayor Stern asked.

"Here he is sir," Susan said and he handed the phone to Mayor Stern.

"Finally," Mayor Stern said.

"Oh my God," Alex yelled out in pain.

"Alex where are you and why are you yelling in my ear? Have you gone mad like everyone else around here?" Mayor Stern demanded to know.

"I am sorry. Mr. Stern, I just spilled my coffee all over my lap when I grabbed my phone," Alex said. "I just stopped for a coffee at Starbucks, Oh no!"

"Oh no? Alex what is wrong"

"Mayor Stern?" Police Chief Cuff asked?

"Yes, who is this? Oh no, it sounds like Police Chief Cuff."

"I don't just sound like her, I am her. Need I remind you and this Coaltonstone boy, tonight of all nights, being New Year's Eve and the never ending Ginger's funeral related events, that I have zero tolerance for talking on phones while driving? In this case I didn't just catch the Coaltonstone boy talking on the phone but drinking coffee too. I have a good mind to arrest him and throw him in the same cell as his brother who is downright miserable right now and we all know how misery loves company. But I am only giving him one warning. Consider the phone hung up."

"What else could go wrong today?" Don Bell asked.

"Don't ask," Susan Jones said. "Don how is your wife?"

"She is okay but there are so many decisions. We never know if we are making the right one. Our family doctors have disappeared so we are getting by with the help of ER docs," Don explained.

"Oh please, we are sorry for your situation, but time is money," Mayor Stern interjected.

"I am sorry. It is all I think about," Don Said.

"I am sorry too," Susan replied.

"So the question is what could possibly go wrong today?"

"As head of Mine Five Safety 'what could possibly go wrong today, is the first question I ask every day," Don Replied.

"Well Mine Five isn't operating anymore and the best houses are being moved to Coalton Valley 2 Where are Jethro and Bill? Weren't they supposed to be helping John with security?" Susan asked.

"I don't know where Jethro and Bill are? I never know where they are. They are technically spies so they are probably spying on the strangers which seem to be everywhere. They could be assisting the cemetery moving-crew. Or they could be assisting in the rounding up of the Undocumented Illegals before they are scattered all over the region. Jethro and Bill are helping with security somewhere and they usual operate under cover and secretly," Don said.

"I certainly hope someone from security is overseeing those two," Mayor Stern said.

"Actually there has been no sighting of Jethro and Bill in Coalton Valley 2. I checked with our people there. I described them. They are not hard to miss. Both of them must be over 6ft 4. There are protestors were camping all around, and even on Cold Feet Mountain chanting and dancing," Susan said.

"I hear that those locals are descendants of Neanderthals," Mayor Stern said.

"We are all descendants of Neanderthals," Susan said.

"Susan, please, silence is golden. Now Don, can you please tell us, one more time, why your brother shot Ginger Goodwin?" Mayor Stern asked without trying to hide his exasperation.

"No, I can't"

"Try!"

"John said it was self defence, sir. I wasn't there, Sir. I have to believe my brother's word but from my own personal experience, I have never known Ginger to be violent or ever owning a gun. I have no idea what happened. I am just as tormented about all this as anyone would be. Ginger was a loyal employee and John is my brother." Don Bell explained.

"Aren't you afraid that you might get mistaken for John, Don, and get shot," Susan asked.

"Susan!" Mayor Stern scolded.

"Of course I am scared. I am terrified. That is why I got my permit to carry a concealed weapon. It was actually John's idea for me to carry one."

"I guess we will just have to wait until John is released from the police station; then he can tell us what actually happened." Susan Jones said.

"John is head of our security, he was just doing his job," Mayor Stern interjected.

"I can't believe my brother would shoot Ginger for no reason, and I can't believe Ginger would have a gun. Ginger hated guns. He should have been given conscientious objector status. This war against the Minese

"G.O.D has declared war on the Minese so every able bodied man was ordered to sign up for service and most of us have, but we also have to differentiate between the Minese Government which we re technically at war with and the actual innocent people who risked their lives to help Ginger out of Mine Five, when our own people could or would not," Don said.

"War always makes everything complicated. And when it is over," Susan said.

"Please, everyone, we need to be focusing on strategy so that the protestors do not get out of hand. This meeting is going to be useless. We don't have our head of security with us, he is in jail. Where is Alex? These protests could get very nasty," Mayor Stern said.

"Actually sir, as I said, the public are participating in Ginger Goodwin's memorial service."

"Susan you mindless fool just shut up. What did I say about talking? I told you to shut up," Mayor Stern screamed as he glared at Susan.

Chapter 3
Lost In A Strange World

December 31st 2030, around 10:00 PM:
Decade II, First Day Of Snowy In The year CCXXXIX of the

Revolution: "Where are we?" Jay asked.

"I wish I knew," Sam said

"Everything I had on me is gone. What are we doing in these striped pajamas?" Kevin asked.

"I still have my father's watch on. It is still working and it lights up amazingly enough. We have two hours left and then this horrible year is over. My headlamp is gone." George replied.

"So we lost a week somewhere? Did we fall into the abys or what?" Jay asked.

"Where ever we are the lighting system is rather cool," Sam said.

"Dangling bulb," George said.

"The light hurts my eyes! Kevin said while the others were glad to see where they were.

"It looks like we fell into a Nazi storage room," George said.

"This stuff looks like a century old," Sam said.

"Yeah, it probably is. Jay said.

"We are obviously somewhere underground," George said.

"Look at all this stuff, what did we fall into?" Sam said as he looked around, feeling miserable.

"I thought all this stuff had been blow up almost a century ago," Sam said.

"Apparently not; it looks like all this stuff has been sitting around waiting until it came back into style," George said.

"We must be in some creepy Nazi cult storage room for. Do you remember anything at all, anyone? Jay asked.

"Last thing I remember is getting hit over the head by something when we were in one of the tunnels trying to help Ginger.

I remember a big Minese guy who said he was going to help us," Kevin said.

"Well where do you think we are?" Jay asked

"Somewhere in a very cold and dark realm," George said

"As in the Reich?" Kevin asked

"Wherever we are it feels like Hell," Jay said.

"I thought Hell was supposed to be hot," Kevin interjected.

"Welcome, to my world, you are in Mina." Ono said as he walked into the room.

"Didn't we meet in one of Mine Five's tunnels? Where are we?" George asked.

"You sloppy men are in one of the many Firestones' storage rooms. You have been sleeping for what you call a week, but we in Mina call a decade. Your friend Ginger Goodwin is dead; shot in cold blood by one of your people, John Bell.

"John shot Ginger? Why would he do that?" George asked.

"John Bell claims self-defense but we say John Bell is a coward and shot a hero, our friend, Ginger Goodwin in cold blood. So in tough times are created by and for tough men. Isn't that right Jethro, Bill any one of you can speak?

Bill and Jethro looked at each other then looked at Ono. Either one of you can answer."

"Yes sir, Sergeant Ono." Jethro and Bill said in unison.

"I remember you two. Weren't you working on John Bell's crowd control team?" George asked.

"We cannot discuss Firestone business with unauthorized personnel," Jethro replied.

"What are you talking about?" Jay said.

"While you drank yourselves silly and jumped into our hemp crate that was being sent with shipment the world has changed drastically in just a mere week, which is why we, in this nation of foresight, have been right all along to call a week a decade.

"What are you talking about? Where are we, really?"

"You are in our underground tunnel system deep underneath the Military Zone. We call our land Mina, but you already must have known that. You have a recall chip in your forehead so that is why you recall nothing."

"What?"

"We discovered you sloppy men in your mess in our hemp crates. We cleaned you up, processed you, under our mandatory recall chip program. This is the way all illegals are processed." Ono said before Jay interrupted him.

"Recall chip? Last thing I remember is being hit over the head with a really hard object. I don't remember anything, and why are we wearing stripped pajamas?"

"You are in the uniform of the illegals. You have no legal identity here. You entered our military zone illegally,"

'Since when did you care about fashion, Jay?" Sam asked.

"Since the word 'fashion' is so close to the word 'fascist', that is when," George retorted back.

"We helped Ginger escape from Safety Chamber E. He refused to fight us in this stupid war you people have raged against us," Ono said.

"Hold on, we are at war?" Kevin asked.

"Yes, and Ginger was shot on the 27th of December, but in our calendar we call December 'Snow' and our New Year is September 22nd, Fall Equinox. Ginger Goodwin refused to sign up to fight us because we were the only ones who actually helped him and because we are all miners," Ono explained.

"That isn't entirely true; before we bumped into you in the tunnel, you were ignoring Ginger's tragic situation just like everyone else was," Jay interjected

"I do not need to argue with you sloppy men. We are not hiding in your world; you are in our hidden world now. Ginger gave a beautiful speech straight from his heart for everyone who would listen. He said it on Pitville's Alternative Radio Station, and was shot minutes later in the heart by heartless men, while he was dying; his son was born and is called James Coaltonstone…"

"What? How could Ginger Goodwin's kid be named after the very man who may have ordered him to be shot?" George asked.

"Boss is a good man. He would not order his son shot and he has adopted his grandson and married Christina. You will be protected here, as long as you obey. Soon Boss will be King of Everything, so we must show respect to him. Baby James was born a few hours after Ginger died. Christina went into labour, and James Coaltonstone woke up the Chief Justice of the Peace so they could marry before baby James was born," Ono explained

"I didn't think Christina was that far along," Jay said.

"No, she was under 22 weeks, actually. James had to coerce the hospital to sell him the life support equipment. Christina was only married to James Coaltonstone for less than a week before she jumped from his ship into icy Arctic waters. Enough gossip.

"Figures, I would do the same if I married James Coaltonstone," Jay said.

"Hold on, is Christina okay, will the baby be okay?" George asked.

"It is not for me to talk about boss's business. I have said too much already. You are now in the militarized zone on my side of the Bering Strait, without a permit. And let me add that you are here very illegally.

"That is terrible English," Jay said.

"So what? It is now you sloppy men who must watch your every step, the tables have been turned.

"I don't understand. What are you talking about? Where are we? Why are we here?" Jay asked

"We need miners. You have been smuggled out of your tunnels into ours," Ono replied.

"But why don't you just keep your miners at home, if you need miners so badly," Sam asked.

"Because the miners want to be paid in American money," Ono explained

"So do we!" Jay interjected.

"Here, you are paid nothing. You work. You live. Pitville chapter of G.O.D. and the Exclusion League, have declared war on the Minese people even though we carried Ginger Goodwin out of the mine, when no one else would. We are good people and before war was declared we were treated like garbage. Now after war is declared we are treated like your enemy even though we are all miners. We find the wealth of the world. Without us, there would be no resources, no fuel nothing. Now you are here, you get to know us. That will be good," Ono said.

"So what else did you bring over to the other side besides us, and how did we lose a week. I find this very hard to believe," Jay asked.

"I told you before what you call a week, we call a decade. To answer your question, which is really none of your business, we brought over anthracite coal of course, hemp, jade and gold. The boss is moving some of the houses in Pitville to Coalton Valley 2 So we will be going back and forth from this base. Boss is also going to melt the Polar Ice Caps a bit so it will be easier to mine up in the Northern Wasteland," Ono explained.

"How is he planning to do that?" Jay asked.

"Knowing Coaltonstone, he is going to nuke them," George said.

"Exactly," Ono replied.

"Wouldn't that melt the ice caps, sooner before later, making the axis tilt and make the climate even more extreme than it already is?" Jay asked.

"We in Mina only look at the positive. We cannot control nature. Climate change happens naturally. Earth changes, we all change. It will be easier to mine everything now. It was too hard to mine what was mineable in that frozen wasteland. We ship out on our new routes. We work under Boss' flag. Once those ice caps are melted we will have a North East Passage to glory, and a new asset to tax," Ono explained.

"Is mineable even a word?" Sam asked.

"Come on Sam," Jay said.

"What about the radiation?" George asked.

"What about it? And why do you mock me, sloppy man in stripped pajamas. One day I will be one of the most powerful generals on this planet, and no one will even remember that you existed at all." Ono responded.

"Well, where we come from radiation is feared just as much as cancer is," George said.

"Radiation? Cancer? We are never told about those things," Jay said.

"It is all natural. Anyway it is Boss' business, not yours. You do as you are told or you will be sorry. And you are now in the Military Zone without a permit," Ono replied. "You will use these tunnels to work and you will be assigned a place to live in the cave district and you must keep it clean. You walk there in these tunnels, you must not litter. These tunnels are your world now. They are black and shiny and have state of the art lighting system. We work a ten hour day and a ten day week."

"You mean you work for ten hours?" Sam asked

"Yes and we have ten hour days. You see our clock; we have ten hours not twelve.

"What?" Jay asked.

"You have a lot to learn about our ways. You can't stay here; we are making very important experiments further north. You will be happy in cave district. You will work. Discover our ways," Ono explained.

"Well what about our wives and kids? We can't just forget them. We need them and they need us," Jay protested.

"You are foolish men. They will soon forget you. They will think you are dead. Christina married Boss the day Ginger was shot. We are at war." Ono said.

"This war is already very stupid and cruel, isn't it?" Jay Paylor added.

"War is stupid when leaders refuse to be reasonable. Now that the ice has thawed enough so that Northern Sea Route is able to change everything, the whole world of power will be turned upside down. No one is going to let that happen without a fight. Of course there will be conflict between haves and not haves," Ono said.

"You mean have nots?" Jay said.

"Yes, 'the have nots'. We are in hidden land of Mina and will prevail. Boss will soon become king of everything. Boss is working with G.O.D. so that we will own the weather and today we own you. We don't pay you but we feed you. If you don't do as we say, exactly, we blow you up. Why are you sloppy men laughing? You, stand by that wall, now." Ono ordered as Sam obeyed. You three stand far away," Ono ordered again as he took out an ancient looking remote control and pushed a button."

"Sam appeared to be burning up in a flame as he disappeared into a pile of dust.

"How did you do that? I mean why did you do that? He did nothing to you." Jay said almost in tears.

"Warning for you, obey. This is a militarized zone. You are lucky that I don't blow you all up. You are nothing but a nuisance to me. Be grateful that I have spared your lives. You owe me your lives. I am your master. These tunnels go to many places, and we will continue digging. You now work for me. You men talk too much. You must be silent to be successful in Mina. You will live in ten hour days and ten day weeks, just like we do. You are in my land. You will live here until you die here."

Ono said as he blew his whistle. Four men in black SS uniforms, complete with swastika armbands and black boots, appeared at the entrance. They kicked their heels and stood to attention while a fifth man wearing a black robe entered the room.

"Sergeant Ono, are you a fool? Your father tells me that you are being trained to replace the Supreme One. Just tell me that you are not a fool," Judge Bell commanded.

"Judge Bell? What are you doing here, are you going to arrest Ono for blowing up Sam?" George asked.

"Actually I should be asking you that question. Judge Bell sounding more irritated than condescending. "You are the ones here illegally in a military zone, you are a fool, only a fool would be here.

"I am not sure how we got here, or where we are, or what happened," George said.

"Why did Ono have to kill Sam? He never hurt anyone," Kevin said.

"Sergeant Ono made a mistake, that will never be repeated," Judge Bell said as he raised his voice.

"Why did Ono have to kill Sam so mindlessly like that, as if he didn't matter to anyone. Sam did matter. He mattered to us and he mattered to his family," George said.

"Ono, did you hear that. You blew someone up who will be missed. You are acting like a fool. Where is your sense of strategy? Your father assures me that you have inherited such a mind. I do not see a strategic mind that is why we admitted you to the Firestones." Judge Bell said.

Chapter 4
Doctor Ashley Knight wonders what to do.

In-Reach Entry, LOG #3, written by Dr. Ashley Knight

December 31st, 2030, Around 10:15 PM: I am not sure what happened to Christina. I am not sure if she tried to commit suicide or if she fell from the ship's deck. One of the ship's staff said that she heard Christina call out Ginger's name and may have seen his projection in the water.

Daniel suspects that it was Jackson, from the PPZ, who stole my patient's InReach files during his and Dianne's visit to my Pitville office. Talking about my Pitville office, I am very concerned that Laura Bell, Don Bell's wife, will feel that I have abandoned her during what could be one of the worst days of her life, because she will be losing her left breast to breast cancer. I am here on this ship just staring at Christina and her little baby who is so small; it is a miracle he is still living. He is quite the fighter. James has shown me medical files where a number of Minese babies who have been born before their time and thriving, a little weaker maybe, but thriving anyway. James swears that the Supreme Being is less rigid with time clocks than we are. First time I saw one of James' ten hour clocks and ten day calendars I thought he was crazy. Now I think he could drive us crazy by disorienting us with this strange way of measuring time. Like everything else, this strange schedule system is self-serving for James. Shorten days by 2 hours, less time to sleep.

Another pressing problem, though it now seems to be a world away, is that the possible misuse of my patient's InReach files by the PPZ cameraman goes against every book of ethics that I can think of. The whole point for my 'InReach Project was to help my clients find their inner strength, their inner diamond, which once found, will enable them to meet any objective or goal of their choosing. I am appalled that anyone would steal my clients' files and then use inside information to create a make believe whistle blower called Deep Coal. And with Ginger Goodwin being Ginger Goodwin, he was assumed to be Deep Coal, which may have been one of the reasons why John Bell shot him. Who knows? I am just devastated so I can imagine what kind of frame of mind Christina was in before she fell from the ship's deck, into that icy Arctic water.

Ginger died too soon on the very day his son was born too soon.

I know my theory works and has the potential to heal. Having the internal strength to face the external world as a stronger and more focused person, is everything. As a humanist psychologist, I do not want to use psychology to dehumanize. I want to use the tools to uplift.

Men create goals and objectives as their birthright and often are given the freedom to do so. But women tend to have their goals cut down before they are obtainable. Especially in Pitville, women are judged, very harshly may I add, by attributes others place on them, not by their accomplishments. And once these unfair judgements get under the skin, I have seen this over and over again, mental distress sometimes leading to chemical changes to their system. Men tend to have it much easier, when it comes to managing their lives by following objectives. Even when a woman has a clear objective, goal and possibly even love for a profession, she is treated as bossy, egotistical, and the busy bodies of Pitville are out in force, pecking her into submission.

To come back to us, Christina needs to feel safe again.

Now baby Ginger, James Coaltonstone has managed to engineer a speedy adoption and has legally called baby Ginger James Coaltonstone Junior. The only reason why they are not referring baby Ginger as Junior, is because Mathew Watson Junior has been called Junior all of his life. Since Mathew

Watson's horrific mining accident, I have advised Christina to rotate the use of the name Junior with Mathew, for obvious reasons.

It is so dark and cold here. We have to dress from head to toe in down suits, parkas and all kinds of layers, especially on our feet and hands, when we go outside. Mathew is actually flyking everywhere. His first photography sale, I believe has helped him to stay on task and move forward with his future, even though he has had terrible tragedies in his life. His father killed in Mine Five, Ginger being shot, both his brother and his mother on life support, and now his name change. James Coaltonstone has managed to defy reason as usual, and for some reason Mathew seems to be still functioning following example's both James and Ginger seem to have taught him. When I left, what I call my patient meeting room, James was showing Mathew a secret handshake he calls the Firestone Shake.

End of In-Reach entry, LOG #3 by Dr. Ashley Knight MD (Coaltonstone Ship).

Chapter 5
Doctor Daniel Smith torn between worlds

In-Reach Entry, LOG #3, written by Dr. Daniel Smith

December 31st, 2030, around 10:15 PM: I don't know where to start. I feel so drained. Baby Ginger is so small, so fragile, and such a little fighter. Ashley fights back tears as she cares for the little guy. Poor Christina; I am still not quite sure what happened. I go from thinking she may have jumped, to she might have fallen. The rumor that she may have been pulled in by Ginger's ghost is totally in bad taste. Anyway Ginger would never do such a thing to a woman he loved so much, and I know she loved him, just as much.

When I delivered Ginger Goodwin, thirty years ago on Christmas day, he was the same way. Anyway the little guy is now legally James Coaltonstone's son and his name is now James Watson-Coaltonstone.

I am certain that Christina Watson suffered from a moment of despair before she jumped into that icy cold Arctic water. James swears that the Supreme Being saved Christina in the same way that he is saving the little baby. I try not to delve into the unexplained since that kind of thing drive me crazy.

What motivates a person to jump from a ship? Christina needs to want to wake up. How can I encourage her to wake up, when all I want to do is sleep away this nightmare too.

That water should be ice. We shouldn't even be this far north on this ship. The ice is being continually zapped by the aerosol guns which are attached to the fleet of ships belonging to the Big Seven Coal Group. This aerosol technology is primitive and barbaric but if that doesn't work, the powers to be are going to nuke the Polar Ice Caps into submission.

Mathew sleeps with his wings on. Everyone around him seems to be dead or almost dead. He has agreed to his name change as long as he could hyphenate Coaltonstone with Watson. Mathew seems to be blocking off his feelings and doing a pretty good job of it. He sold some of his photography to that creepy cameraman from PPZ, Jackson Green. Speaking of Jackson Green, I am certain that he was the one who stole Ashley's project data; leaked it, called the whistleblower 'Deep Coal', and made people think it was Ginger Goodwin.

My guess is that John Bell will be out of jail and about as if nothing happened any moment now, and so will Bobby, which will only motivate the unemployed miners to rebel, maybe even violently.

Talk about violent, I thought it would be serene here, despite the bitter cold and darkness, there are a lot of loud explosions and cracking sounds. Mathew Junior told me that when he was flyking he saw a lot of run down boats that looked like protestors were heading here and that we might be getting tracked. So who knows what the future will bring.

And who can blame them? Rebelling is the preferable option to suicide I suppose.

The new town is going to be even more depressing than the old town and should be called Machiavelli Valley 2 instead of Coalton Valley 2. And this obsession with ten hour clocks and ten day weeks is just beyond belief. I have seen my share of Machiavellian personalities in my day, but James Coaltonstone beats them all. To use ten hour clocks and ten day weeks to manipulate and confuse people will also stretch the work day and work week, leaving little time for much else.

I think Christina and Ginger's baby will be okay. He is a little fighter. And only time I see any softness in James is when he places faces with the baby. I have never seen him like that before. He is both grandfather and father to the little guy which is a very strange situation. I hear rumors that James was glad to see Ginger shot, but I find it hard to believe that any man would want his son dead, even a son he refused to acknowledge, yet he has taken to the baby as if it were his own, technically he is his grandson, he seems to be acknowledging that in a roundabout way.

Poor Christina; I am still not quite sure what happened. I go from thinking she may have jumped, to she might have fallen. The rumor that she may have been pulled in by Ginger's ghost is totally in bad taste. Anyway Ginger would never do such a thing to a woman he loved so much, and I know she loved him, just as much.

I hear that Jackson Green and Dianne Black will be coming aboard soon to celebrate New Year's Eve. I must have a talk with Jackson, but I am not sure how to go about it.

End of In-Reach entry, LOG #3 by Dr. Daniel Smith MD (Coaltonstone Ship).

Chapter 6
Looking For The Coalton Ship

December 31st 2030; around 11:00 PM: "I can see the Coaltonstone Ship on the tracker," Jackson announced.

"Wonderful," Dianne replied. "I wonder what Coaltonstone is planning to do?

"We know that he is moving buildings from Pitville to a flat spot near Cold Feet Mountain and he will be calling his new mining town Coalton Valley 2. We also know that coal mining is already an ongoing concern at that location. No one is on strike there, and the mountain is full of coal. I have heard rumors, but they sound crazy, even for Coaltonstone," Jackson said.

"What rumors?" Dianne asked.

"Coaltonstone is alleged to be involved in the nuking of the polar ice caps, so he can free up the natural resources now stuck under all that ice, and create new shipping lanes." Jackson explained.

"You are right, that is crazy."

"That is one of the rumors," Jackson said.

"Okay, what is the other rumor?" Dianne asked.

"Well if it is true it is a big one. The radioactive waste is buried all over the place, and some of it might be leaking. They just seem to dig holes, making it look like it is a burial, since that location is a cemetery, and bury these containers of radioactive waste.

"Where is the waste come from/"

"I would guess that it is from the polar ice melting project. Now they have to move it all to make room for Coalton Valley 2. If that is not bad enough, he is trying to push the natives from their ancestral land, Frozen Feet Mountain.

"We are already hearing eskimos swearing that the sky is changing. The sun sets and rises slightly differently than the old days. They are attributing the change to jet trails, melting of the Polar Ice Caps, and the tilting of the axis.

"Dianne you are looking ravishing in your down suit, permission to board Ship One is granted. Just come aboard when you are ready." James said then added "Doctor Smith just sent me an email; he wants to talk to Jackson, man to man about some sort of dysfunction that he appears to have,"

"What? I don't have any dysfunction," Jackson said louder than he intended to.

"Oops," James said wondering what the message was really about.

Chapter 7
Mina's cave district

January 1ˢᵗ, 2031, around 1:30 AM Pitville Time: Decade II, Second day of Snowy in the Year CCXXXIX of the Revolution: "Well here we are; home away from home. What are we supposed to do now? Jay asked.

"You sloppy men do what you always do. You make some Mr. Noodles and tea then you should go to sleep.

"That is not what we usually do. We usually have a beer and a dish of Mr. Noodles," Jay said.

"You have two hours less to waste in sleep. You have no Sunday here. You should thank the Supreme Being for the gift of work. Eat, sleep, wake up when the bot whistle whistles, go to work like usual," Ono blared from a loud speaker which was situated in the corner of the small cave room.

"Wow, is this even real?" Jay asked.

"I would think so, Jay. You are never in my dreams," George replied.

"So do we have a plan at all?

"You eat, sleep and go to work on Boss Whistle's command and nothing more. Death is your only escape from here." Ono sounded angrier this time as he blared from the speaker.

Chapter 8
Mathew's Homework Problem

December 31st 2030, around 11:30 PM: "It is half an hour before New Year's Eve and you are doing homework? I am not sure if I should hug you or ostracize you?"

"Maybe you can help me; I am really confused about this history assignment. I don't get it," Mathew complained.

"And you think I should get it? Tell me why?

"Well you were born four years after the Kennedy's assassination so don't you remember why they kept so many files secret and they just opened them up last year?" Mathew asked.

"How would I know? It was all secret and I was busy flittering my youth away playing with super balls, yoyos, toy robots and slinkies.

"So how am I supposed to answer the question?" Mathew asked.

"Well, what is the question?"

"There are a few. Why did JFK get assassinated, why were files only opened last year, and what color of dress was Jackie Kennedy wearing at the time.

"Jackie's dress was pink. You must have known that answer. It is hard to know why JFK was assassinated. Lee Harvey Oswald allegedly shot him, but popular thoughts seem to ride with he had help or he may have been a decoy. It was a terrible thing. He was so young with so much promise and maybe that is why someone wanted him shot. Who knows why people shoot other people. Some people think just because a person owns a gun or two makes them want to shoot it, unstable people anyway, normal people won't feel like that. Normal people like us."

"So why was it so secret? Why did they open the files up last year?" Mathew asked.

"Nobody really knows. Some say it might have been just to cool down speculation but by making files secret only made people more curious in my opinion," James explained.

"What about Pay Of Pigs?"

"Sometimes Presidents have to choose between the least evil, and the decision is almost never a winning choice. At the time, Russia had missiles so close to us, we were terrified. Somethings, especially in politics, have no answer.

Chapter 9
Threats

January 1st 2031, around 10:00 AM: "I am holding this meeting because ever since the Warner report has been declassified, concerning cold war secret technology, the more radical miners have found a way to acquire an electromagnetic bomb which would cause mass destruction to our electronic equipment. The end result to our assets would be comparable to being attacked by bolts of lightning," John Bell said.

"My God, are you sure?" Mayor Stern asked.

"Almost, we always knew declassifying those reports would be a security risk," John Bell replied.

"Well it sounds rather farfetched to me," Mayor Stern said.

"No the threat is real and the weapon is very portable. Electromagnetic Pulse generators are getting easier to build. And considering how much copper wire has gone missing lately, I think we must remain vigilante," John Bell said.

"When does it end? Was it really necessary to shoot Ginger? The miners are really protesting the shooting," Don Bell said.

"Maybe, but many of our best employees are moving their houses as we speak and joining Coalton Valley 2 at the foot of Cold Feet Mountain. And that is what we should be doing with our time. A lot of preparation is going into this move. We have moved the cemetery and the waste piles which have been contained in safe containers."

"We also have to consider the chaos being caused as the ice caps are being nuked. Part of the fall out is ionization, but the effect seems very minimal where we are," Don said.

"Pitville is old and tired and our coal seam is burning. We are much better off leaving this nightmare behind us." John Bell said.

Chapter 10
Cold Feet Mountain

In-Reach Entry, LOG #1, written by Don Bell
Coalton Valley 2, Hut 7

January 5th 2031, around 10:30 PM: I am here.
Coalton Valley 2 is quite amazing. Considering how long it took
for Coalton Valley 1 to develop, it is like Coalton Valley 2
sprung up overnight. James has assured us that all the radiation
has been cleaned up, though I am not quite sure how that was
done. The radiation counts have been tested and all three times
they have been found to be safe. There are a lot of protestors
sitting by little fires beside little tents.

Mr. Coaltonstone sent my brother to the other side of the
Bering Strait so he can learn how they handle the protestors who
are going on about dump radioactive materials in the Bering Sea.
Actually it is alleged to have happened a long time ago, but it is
just recently that so many cases of cancer have come to public
attention.

There is a lot of commotion outside. I am always getting
mistaken for my brother. I am still not sure what happened or
why John shot Ginger, the whole situation is pretty hard to
understand. Ginger didn't even own a gun. Ginger was one of the
very few people around here who didn't carry a gun.

There are lots of people around my house. I think they are protesting as if I was the one who shot Ginger, and it wasn't me. I still can't figure out how it happened.

End of In-Reach entry, LOG #1 by Don Bell (Coalton Valley 2, Hut 7)

Chapter 11
Warming The Arctic

January 6th 2031, around 10:30 AM: "Hello loyal viewers, this is Dianne Black, up in the very cold and dark Coalton Valley 2.

We are here to report the very sad and senseless shooting of Don Bell, who, we believe had been mistaken for his brother, John Bell who, as head of security for James Coaltonstone's Mine Five, part of the Big Seven Goal Group, is alleged to have shot Ginger Goodwin. John Bell claims self-defense. While working at Mine Five, Don Bell mostly functioned in the capacity of Safety Manager for the mine, though sometimes he did assist his brother in security matter. Ginger Goodwin was Don Bel's assistant and was considered a hero after he prevented the morning crew from descending into Mine Five, only minutes before the December 22nd explosion, which James Coaltonstone's son, Bobby was found negligent and presently serving twenty-six year sentence of hard labor working in one of many Penal Colonies located in the Arctic Mine District.

Don Bell was transferred to the Coalton Valley 2 only days earlier and was to work in a supervisory role while the installation of assets, many of which have been transported from Pitville.

Chapter 12
The weather Is Not ours to change

January 6th 2031, around 12:30 PM: "So here we are Mathew living the dream. All dressed up, with Beautiful Dianne and her cameraman and you need to pay attention, so you can learn as much as you can from Jackson," James said as he looked over Jackson's camera to make that is his hair was combed over correctly.

"Actually Mathew could teach me a lot. He has an amazing eye for photography," Jackson replied.

"Now look at all these incredible ice sculptures, talk about luck. What do you think the chances are that a Supreme Being managed to carve all these pieces?" James asked.

"The Arctic is so vast and these Ice Sculptures are incredible but why are talking about a supreme being. I would have never thought of you being a religious or superstitious man, James," Dianne said.

"I suppose that I am still in shock that someone would actually kill Don Bell. He was a great safety manager," James said.

"Everyone is getting shot. Uncle James, when do you think they will shoot you?"

"Never,'

"They shot JFK, they shot Ginger, they shot Don, who else do you think will they shoot?"

"No one can really know these things. So as you can see we have a route here, and we are not the only ship. We usually dock at the work camp and the shipping containers pick up whatever they happen to be mining," James explained. Just think what is under all this ice, once we get to it, we, I mean me, will be richer than anyone's wildest dreams," James said.

"Are you going to build a new town here Uncle James?"

"Certainly not, we are going to warm things up and then try to build in the ground where it is warmer and less wind, and then we will build tunnels to connect to the harbors. Mina is a land of tunnels. They are safe, they are warm enough in the winter, cool enough in the summer, and they let the miners live right where they work," James explained.

"I guess that makes a lot of sense since Mina is on ten hour days and ten day weeks, they save time by not having to commute," Mathew said.

"Exactly," James said.

"Do families live in these cave like dwellings too?" Dianne asked.

"Yes, some do, some prefer to live on the surface. But out here you don't find many families, mostly just work crews," James explained.

"What happens if Earth's Axis changes tilt, will it affect us in a drastic way?"

"It might help us warm things up," James said. "If the change does affect the seasons we will just have to adjust. If the change affects the sky you will just have more interesting things to take pictures of, right? There are a lot of positive things which could come out of this melting of ice. That is why I am helping it along a bit, and I am sure that I am not the only one. We will just have to monitor everything very carefully from a distance. Dianne did you know that I will be donating a few wind mills and solar energy panels to those tiny settlements that are scattered about," Coaltonstone revealed.

"No I didn't know that. Such a thoughtful gift would make those people's lives a bit easier, I would think," Dianne replied.

"That is what I thought. I am not that concerned about the

axis changing tilt. If it added to the extremeness of the weather patterns I would just have to get the authorities to round up more deportees and prisoners to work the mines that are located in hostile locations or may have a bit of radioactivity leaking," James explained.

Chapter 13
Flying around

"As you can see Dianne, while Pitville is going bust, there is a boom going on big time in Arctic Coal mining. As the Polar Ice Caps melt there will be more shipping lanes, more prosperity and most importantly, more happiness," James said.

"So when is the next nuclear explosion so you can melt more of the Polar Ice Cap?" Jackson asked.

"What are you talking about?" James said as he winked.

"Don't you think it is rather pathological to be nuking the Polar Ice Caps for material gain?" Jackson asked.

"And you think using this technology to blow up cities is less pathological?" James shot back.

"You are evading Jackson's point," Dianne interjected.

"You better believe I am," James replied. "Now, Dianne, I am sure it is obvious by now I am giving you an incredible opportunity to see the vastness of the Arctic. The best way to see the Arctic and my little oil wells, is to fly over them. The Arctic is the last frontier to explore, besides space, I suppose. As you can see... Hold on, there is a polar bear, quick get my rifle Mathew."

"You are not going to shoot it are you? Polar bears are pretty much endangered and that one isn't hurting anyone," Mathew said.

"What do you think Dianne, do you think I should shoot

the polar bear?"

"Absolutely not, James, please don't," Dianne begged.

"You are kidding, right Uncle James. You would never shoot a polar bear, unless it was in self-defense, right?"

"Jackson are you getting good shots? If it is a female she probably has cubs nearby," Dianne said.

"I am getting great shots."

"How did I find myself in a plane with a bunch of protesting environmentalists? It is the story of my life," James complained.

"You are having a good life; why not let the polar bear just live his or her life.

Chapter 14
Melting Ice Cap opens shipping lanes

"So what do you see when you look around, Mathew?" James asked

"I guess I see all kinds of oil drilling rigs and shipping containers," Mathew replied.

"And what else?" James asked.

"Fishing boats; I see lots and lots of fishing boats. I don't see many people on some of those boats." Mathew replied.

"Well people running fishing boats and oil rigs are pretty passé," James explained.

"I know what I see," Dianne interjected. "I see flags, lots and lots of flags. And all those flags are waving in the wind representing all the countries who want to break this all up. And the weird thing is all these rigs are so close to each other, yet they never seem to collide as if they all belong in parallel universes.

"Not yet anyway," James said.

"What do you mean not yet anyway?" Mathew asked.

"All these rigs and ships and flags haven't collided yet. I suppose right now they are satisfied with colluding with each other. I guess it is just a matter of time when all these interests conflict. The million dollar question is when.

"So is it true that a fifth of the earth's oil may be under all this and the Arctic is as big as Africa? Mathew asked.

"Pretty much; if all the countries that claim a stake in all this try to carve it up they may make it even more chaotic than it is right now," James said.

"Well it doesn't seem chaotic at all right now," Mathew said.

"Exactly, wait until the regulators takeover. Mathew you are witnessing history. One day all this ice on this ocean could be gone. And then it might seem to us more of an estuary than an actually ocean so that the most powerful will gain control of the expanding shipping routes and the least powerful may feel scorned and act like saboteurs," James explained.

"And that is why I hate politics," Jackson said.

"Well, the beauty of this situation right now is that there isn't any regulation. Soon this wild crazy place will be micromanaged to death, and anyone doing anything will be intimidated by the slippery arms of bureaucracy, ready to grab whatever it can in fees and taxes," George grumbled.

"How much tax do you pay, Mr. Coaltonstone?" Dianne asked.

"As little as I can dear, and you know why? Because I am smart. Why should I pay into a system which only grows more slippery arms to grab whatever it can from me and people like me, so they can just give it to unemployed bums. The system is set up just to intimidate and get its mob rule policies in place, then everything you try to do is stopped in its tracks accept the slippery arm that charges exuberant fees to let you apply to something that you are eligible for but don't qualify for. One is either forced to give before one even starts or one has to find a way to get around the entire aggravating mess." James snorted while he took a breath.

"I totally disagree with you," Jackson said.

"You would," James retorted. "You are working because you are funded by public money. All those bums that are getting in my way whenever and wherever I turn live only because they get public money. If it was up to me, I would have every single one of them shot the way that general in the south does. We don't need all those people ruining everything. My bots serve mankind politely and don't ever demand anything back when I ask them to do simple things. Coalton Valley 2 is going to be as automated as possible. We are going to have most of our coal transported by driverless trucks, and you will see how fast and efficient my town will be compared to Coalton Valley 1. And will all these new shipping lanes being opened up between North America and Eurasia, there will be an infinite demand for my coal,"

"But what happens to all those people who lose their jobs when they are replaced by your bots," Mathew asked.

"Shoot them if they can't adapt to the modern world. Shoot them before they breed even more malcontents," James retorted.

"

Chapter 15
Using Disputed Arctic Routes

"Why would anyone call my technology pathological? James asked looking hurt. "Mina has a right to use these new shipping routes just like any other country has that right. We are in a new era and we should be enjoying it. The Arctic is just a remnant of an old Ice Age, and who wants to go back to that?" James said defenselessly.

"Uncle James, it is just an article," Mathew said feeling guilty for his unintentional betrayal of his new step father.

"No it is not just an article. The Pitville Times rag is using my favorite step son's photographs. That is not what I was expecting from you."

"Well I actually sold the photos to Jackson and he sold them to different places. Jackson gives me royalties and then I send most of the money back to Grandma Watson," Mathew explained.

"How is your grandmother doing?"

"Not good and not bad. She is renting out the backyard to a couple who are expecting a baby."

"Are those people protestors, and are they planning to have the baby delivered in the backyard?

"I don't know. Grandma refuses to rent out my room t and she wants me to come back home as soon as I can. My guess is that the couple camping outside may rent my room if they decide to stay, and I will have a good reason to build the tree house that I have always wanted," Mathew said looking for a clue to how James really was feeling.

"That plan makes sense. You love flyking why wouldn't you want to nest in a tree like a bird,"

"Uncle James!"

"I don't see why your grandma doesn't move in with us," James said. "Does she still blame me for Mathew's death? The way she goes on about it you would think I set deliberately set up that boss bot to cause the accident. And the key word here is accident. It was all an accident," James said.

"I think Grandma understands that it was an accident but I think she wishes that you would have apologized more, instead of just offering everyone money and then disappearing," Mathew said.

"We can't keep looking backwards, Mathew or we will be not further ahead than all those losers we left behind in Pitville," James said.

Chapter 16
Melting Polar Ice Caps

"More pictures, more insults," James complained.

"You can't blame me for the article. Jackson says that if articles were positive they would never sell newspapers, Mathew protested.

"But you took the money didn't you?" James said accusingly.

"And you wouldn't have if you had been me?"

"You took credit for picture and I see you just use Watson in your byline not Watson Coaltonstone," Mathew said feeling even more guilty than he had before.

"I have been using Watson as my last name all my life, I just feel funny using Coaltonstone as part of my last name," Mathew said feeling very guilty.

"When I was fifteen I was making my own decisions too. That is what men do. You don't need to be apologizing to me for any decision you make, Mathew. You are the one who will have to live with the consequences," James said.

"Well it was the bot that calls himself IQ who made the decision," Mathew interjected.

"You are making that bot sound human. First of all how can a bot call himself anything at all? It is impossible for any bot to just make a decision like climbing up a tree to make friends with the one and only Mathew Watson-Coaltonstone. The bot gets the order somehow and then acts upon it, James asked.

"I don't know, he just introduced himself to me as IQ and asked me if I would like to be his friend," Mathew explained.

You were using my state of the art bot to lift you in the air to click a button on your camera to take that photo even though the explosion was supposed to be kept totally secret,"

"I didn't ask the bot to help me. He just climbed up into my tree house and we started talking and that is when we both saw the little mushroom cloud in the distance."

"I am not saying that I don't believe you Mathew, since you have never lied to me, so I don't have any cause to think that you would like to me, but your story is unbelievable," James said.

"I don't know why you say this is unbelievable; you are the one who goes on about artificial intelligence more than anyone else I have ever known," Mathew replied.

"But it is a theory. I always mean in theory," James retorted.

"Can't I just tell you what happened?" Mathew begged.

"I thought that was what you were doing, with or without my permission. And as I said before, when I was your age, I was my happiest when I did things my way," James said hoping that his tone was sounding a little more pleasant than it had been.

"I didn't take do this my way, the bot did. IQ just picked me up and I just clicked and I got this picture. And then he put he jumped out of the tree holding on to me, and then I got an email from Jackson asking me if I had any new photographs, and I sent him that one. It was almost like Jackson could see me or something," Mathew said feeling a little embarrassed that his story sounded so crazy.

"I believe what you are saying is what you believe to be true. And let us leave it at that. Who knows what happened to that bot when it was with Goodwin trapped in the Safety Chamber. When it comes to Ginger and technology, anything could happen," James said.

"You are not saying that you think Ginger is living in IQ," Mathew said.

"Of course I am not saying that," James retorted.

"Anyway the bot is really friendly and loves reciting

passages out of the Rights Of Man to me when he visits me in my tree house," Mathew said.

"Those are guard bots, not data bots or photograph taking bots. I guess you know I know Ginger found a copy of Rights of Man in Safety Chamber E and read it to the bot, foolish thing to do," James said wishing that Ginger was still around so he could scold him for his foolishness.

"The bot just stood out on the ground and took the photo during the blast; you have to admit it is pretty amazing. You can see that explosion in space on the ground. This darkness is good for something. We see everything in the night sky but not much on the ground unless we have fires, flares, electric lights.

Chapter 17
James Is Being Criticized

"Good morning James," IQ said as he moved pieces on a chess board. Mathew forced himself out of bed.

"Good morning sleepy head, that was quite a climb up into your little fort in a tree. I brought you a housewarming present," James said as he placed the scales beside the chess board.

"You didn't need to bring me a present but it is really nice that you did," Mathew said.

"I really think that you needed these scales more than I do. These scales of balance will remind you, whenever you look at them, what it means to be a Coaltonstone and a Firestone," James explained.

"Is something wrong?" Mathew wondered out loud.

"There certainly is, as James placed a very thin newspaper on the table. Another article criticizing me, and what should be above the article, a photograph that you took of a polar bear which appears to be drowning, and in the background, hundreds of minese walking to work, wearing helmets with flashlights duct taped to them, complete with lunch pails in hand. Yes something is very wrong. I do not think these criticisms are fair. These failing newspapers are using me to sell newspapers and I resent this exploitation very much," James complained.

"But Uncle James you brought all those deported Minese out here. You set them up in houses that used to belong to people living in Pitville," Mathew protested.

"That is wrong. Those houses belong to me, the miners only live in those houses while they are employed. When they are no longer employed by my mine, for whatever reason, then I have a right to evict them. That is the law and the nature of the world. Those people will find somewhere to stay," James said as he tried to reassure Mathew, that things have always been this way.

"Jackson told me that a lot of the miners are living in the campgrounds near town," Mathew said.

"Not that horrible place that floods all the time, where we send out of towners," James asked.

"Yes that is the one. It floods all the time," Mathew said.

"That is why I offered to build a wall. A security wall could keep some of the water out, and people who might boat by won't have to feel offended when they see poor people.

Chapter 18
Pitville Times compares
James Coaltonstone to Hitler

"How could anyone compare me to Hitler," James said looking hurt.

"I don't know, the papers do it all the time."

"Mathew, you are not helping," James retorted.

"I meant they are calling people Hitler all the time. Not just you, that guy in the south is being referred to as Hitler too, all the time. That is what I meant," Mathew said.

" I don't think it is fair either Uncle James. I mean those people who are working for you are not complaining, so whose business is it of anyone's what you pay those people? They are not supposed to be in this country. They came here to mine. So that is what they are doing," Mathew said.

"Exactly, there is a war on, we need resources, the Minese can't be let go right now, because they could use information and other secrets against us but I am not institutionalized a holocaust. It will cost billions to move millions of illegals; so if illegals are in this country they need to pay their way. And those people don't have anything to lose the way I do. If I lost everything, I would be worse off than them, because I would be in debt for at least $10 billion dollars. You know what this like son. Having that clock ticking overhead, compound minute by minute, what does anyone know about that.

I may be one of the richest men on the planet, but I am also one of the most indebted. I am King of Coal, but imagine if they started to call me King of debt. Can you just imagine those robo calls coming in every second, tying up all my phones, demanding money now, or else. What do those people know about that?"

"Uncle James it is okay," Mathew said as he gave James a hug. "I understand a lot more than people think I do. Just because I am a kid, flyking around as if I didn't have a care in the world, like a bird, doesn't mean I have a bird-brain. Now that we are staying in Coalton Valley 2, do you think I could build a tree house in that big tree in the back yard," Mathew asked.

"I don't know. You are flyking around a lot; you hang out in trees a lot. Are you sure if I let you build a tree house you will still socialize with us who live on the ground," James said.

"Uncle James, if I get a tree house, you would be always welcome," Mathew said.

Chapter 19
G.O.D Shuts Down Coaltonstones' Disposal Wells.

"They just came here, without an appointment, they handed me this piece of paper ordering me to close down over two thousand disposal wells that I own," James said as he slammed his coffee cup down on the table, making some of the chess piece roll onto the floor with such force they bounced and then fell out of Mathew's tree house.

"Uncle James, you have to calm down," Mathew said as he motioned for IQ to get their check pieces.

"Your blood pressure must be through the roof Mr. Coaltonstone," IQ said.

"IQ get those check pieces, please," Mathew begged.

"Do you know what I could lose now?" James asked.

"I don't know, I suppose a lot," Mathew said.

"No, more than a lot. I could lose everything," James whimpered. "Everything, while the interest on the interest compounds second by second.

"I know how you feel, Uncle James," Mathew said.

"No you don't. How could you possibly know how I feel," As he pushed the table, Mathew was pushed into IQ who was just climbing up the ladder with the chess pieces,"

"Oh My God, Mathew, I am so sorry," James said.

"It is okay, IQ caught me," Mathew said.

"Sir, Mathew has lost his father when he was a child, his mother has been in a coma since the evening of December 29th.

Mathew's baby brother was only 2 days old at the time when his mother became comatose. That little baby has lost more than he or anyone will ever know. He will try thing as he gets older and everything will be much harder for him than mostly everyone else he knows. He might face a life of rejection and daily challenge. The only saving grace that protects that tiny guy is that he doesn't know yet how fragile his life really is. He doesn't know that he is defying death with every breath he takes. He doesn't know what it means to be what he is; an extreme preemie with less than 22 weeks in gestation. And while in gestation, before that state was rudely interrupted, he lost his father, and that little baby is now having to learn to lie in a fetal position, and does he cry? No. It is Doctor Knight who cries. The day Ginger was shot, Mathew lost a man who was partly his best friend and partly a surrogate father. Sir I think you owe both Mathew and his little brother a sincere apology," IQ said.

"No, it is Okay. Really," Mathew said.

"I am sorry Mathew. I really am. I know you have lost a great deal too and so has your little brother,"

"Yes, but Uncle James you saved his life. You have to see both sides of everything or you will drive us and everyone else nut," Mathew said as he tried to hug James.

"You just don't understand how serious this will be. I could lose everything, I mean everything. Everything is tied into everything. What I could lose could be huge. I just don't think those G.O.D. members have a clue. They said that they think that my wells contributed to some obscure earthquake in some God forsaken place that no one will ever care about. They said they suspect. They don't even know for sure. What I could lose is huge. And when I mean huge I do mean huge. All my assets are interconnected and intertwined with each other, because they are all used as collateral for all my projects. When one of my assets is taken out of my stack of assets, it could be like a whole house of cards falling down, not just on me, but on everyone who depends on me," James said as he was trying not to panic. "And besides that it is embarrassing. Those numbskulls from G.O.D. don't have anything close to what I have to lose. Do they know what it will cost me to have all my wells shut down? The domino effect will be huge, just huge. And just because an earthquake has upset some Eskimos living in igloos or whatever they live in these days," James said as he pouted his face was turning red.

"It will just take a minute, roll up your sleeve and I will make sure that your blood pressure is in the normal range," IQ said.

"What kind of bot are you? Stop ordering me about! I am the one who is supposed to be ordering you about," James said. "What is wrong with everyone? I am the one who is supposed to be giving out orders, and today all I am getting is orders from faceless bureaucrats and now from a stupid bot."

While James was yelling Mathew was sure he just saw a tear drop falling down his cheek.

Chapter 20
Cold Feet Mountain Walks

March 15th 2031, around 4:00 AM: "Deep Coal is angry. Cold Feet Mountain is about to roll. Run everyone run," IQ said as loud as his hardware allowed.

"Jackson, can you hear me," Dianne yelled through the door.

"Of course I can hear you. You are yelling at me through the door. Is it time to get up already? I thought I just fell asleep."

"Something awful is happening. I think it is an earthquake or something. Can't you feel it. It sounds like the mountain is roaring but that is impossible. Get up Jackson. Can you hear me? Get up; we got to get out of here."

"Wait, I have my earphones on."

"Can you hear me? Hurry!"

"I am not sure if I am hearing what you were hearing. I am hearing a lot of screaming.

"Hurry, Jackson. We have to get out of here, something is happening to the mountain,"

"What? Why are you bitching at me so early in the morning. It is 4:10 AM,"

Jackson grabbed his huge duffel bag that was already full with towels belonging to the hotel, his camera, phone and wallet. He grabbed the van keys from the table and left everything else behind. Dianne had already grabbed her purse and house coat. They ran through the empty hotel hallway hand in hand. They ran down the stairs and through the glass doors as fast they could. They jumped into the van and were thankful that the road was as empty as the hotel's hallways. How they managed to drive away in the nick of time, they would never know. The mountain came tumbling down and buried the west side of Coalton Valley 2 which included the bank, the hotel and twenty-five huts. The roar of the mountain was deafening.

"Don't look back Di."

"We are journalists."

"Yes, but we aren't heroes. We can look back later."

"All those people buried. It was lucky you were awake, what were you doing?"

"I was having a bit of an argument with Coaltonstone on Twitter. Then I heard a voice coming from somewhere yelling that Deep Coal was angry. We were both deleting our tweets while laughing at each other. We started around 3:00 AM. It started with a comment from him about my past loves in war zones. Then I could feel the earth shaking, and right after we escaped from there that awful noise. And seconds later everything there seems to be gone. The bank, the hotel and those little cottages, they are all gone.

"You know Di, I would have still been in there, it happened all so fast,"

"Yeah, you lucked out, I was about to leave you there, after you accused me of bitching. I am the boss you know. If I were a man would you call me a bitch? Of course not.

"I am sorry."

"Where are your clothes besides those disgusting underwear?" Dianne asked.

"I suppose they are all under the rubble. I put all the important stuff in the duffle bag. Everything is gone. It happened so fast. We need to get out of this dust. Where should we go, Di?"

"Drive East I suppose until you see something open. A donut shop or something. You will have to put on my spare wardrobe until we get you some clothes."

Chapter 21
Coaltonstone Visits Cold Feet Mountain

March 15th 2031, around 5:45 AM: " W hat do you mean Cold Feet Mountain just fell on the west side of Coalton Valley 2 and the men trapped in the mountain are probably dead?" James asked.

"Sir, it was the most massive rock slide in Tut Island's history. The wedge that was hanging broke away and an estimated 90 million tons of liquid rock came down in seconds and crushed the west side of Coalton 2," David Bell said.

"And there was no warning?"

"Just the usual tremors we feel in the cave every day. Hold on there was a report that some of the survivors heard a voice screaming around 4:00 in the morning, that Deep Coal was angry and everyone needed to evacuate. That was ten minutes before the actual slide which happened in seconds,"

"Who was it?" James asked.

"We don't know. I suppose people thought he was a drunk," Dave said.

"There is an estimated ninety people buried in the rubble and maybe another twenty men buried in the mine. The railway track is gone but the train was saved. A young man was able to run around the rock and flag down the train before it crashed into the slide, sir. Our mining operation's entrance is buried in rock and we must assume that the men trapped inside are dead, or for all managerial purposes, will be dead soon. Most of those men were just deportees, sir. The area has been yellow ribboned," Dave said.

"So your train still has a human driver?" Dianne and Jackson asked at the same time.

"Of course it does."

"Can your driverless technology respond to random human hand signals, in a situation like this?"

"Obviously not in the same way humans can communicate to each other. . The boss bots usually are the ones who control and communicate to our trains," James replied.

"What would have happened if the train had been driverless and a human tried to stop the train with nothing more than just hand signals?" Dianne asked.

"Now, Dianne you know how I hate to speculate when I am speaking to the press."

Chapter 22
Coalton Valley 2 Disaster

March 15th 2031; around 5:55 AM: "This is Dianne Black, with the PPZ, reporting live from the Coalton Valley 2 Disaster at the very foot of Cold Feet Mountain. Good morning and thank you for joining me. I just had the shock of my life. I heard a voice ordering us to run, and I woke up Jackson who was sleeping in another room, in the same hotel. I mean we were sleeping separately but close by.

"It is okay, Dianne, we understand and thank God you are okay and may I say that you both look stunning in your housecoats, but you must be cold." Steve said. "Please carry on."

"Thank you Steve If it weren't for Jackson, I could have been under the rubble. Steve, I owe you my life."

"Hold on Di, you were the one that woke me up. So I think it is I, who owe you my life."

"Look you two, you are both sounding incredibly traumatized and look incredibly cold. I feel cold just looking at you. At least Di has her slippers and house coat on but you Jackson you are wearing a super tiny house coat and it looks very girlish,"

"Obviously it is Di's spare housecoat, I don't waste space carrying housecoats or pajamas when I am on assignment, Steve," Jackson replied.

"Can you go on?

"Certainly, as you know I am a war correspondent, and have had many near misses during my career. I have been to many war and death zones over the years, but today was supposed to be a celebration so as you can see we were not prepared for such a disaster. But no one ever is, unless they are called to one. Let us see if we can get a closer look. Sir, thank you so much. A kind man has just handed Jackson a beautiful parka and matching boots and even a pair of socks.

"Di, take a break come back in five," Steve ordered from the PPZ office thousands of miles away.

"Dear viewers, after these important messages from our sponsors we will be back with a closer look at this tremendous rock slide which some experts believe could be close to 90 million tons of liquid rock which has buried the Western Edge of Coalton Valley 2, including the only bank."

"Quick Jackson; we have five minutes for you to put on those boots and coat and walk to the edge of the rock slide,"

"Di, what is that?"

"Where?"

"Up there, in all that dust?"

"It looks like a giant eagle taking photographs. No, only person that I know who would be taking photographs in a flyke suit is Mathew Watson."

"Mathew? What is he doing here, I thought he told me that he was going to stay with his grandmother for a while," Dianne said.

"He always tells me that too, but something tells me that his grandmother would not be allowing him to flyke around taking photographs as he pleases, dropping in on classes through his computer as he pleases, and making money selling some pretty incredible photos. That part his grandmother probably would be happy with but never would admit it. He was probably here for the same reason that we were all here; to celebrate the opening of Coalton Valley 2, and now look, so much has been lost," Jackson said. Feeling more numb than cold.

"Let's get closer."

"Phone him," Dianne ordered. "Tell him to get down here on the double. What would his mother think?" Dianne said.

"His mother is fighting her own battle," Jackson said.

"We are live," Steve said. "Why aren't you dressed, Jackson."

"Thank God," Jackson said.

"I mean we are on the air," Steve clarified.

"The Watson boy is up there flyking, taking photos. We are zooming in on him," Jackson replied.

"Let me look," Dianne ordered. "Oh my God, I can see people's hands, and heads. Everything is so horrible; I just want to close my eyes to make it all go away."

"I really need to take a break Steve. It is all getting to me now," Dianne said before she collapsed.

Chapter 23
Mystery Around Rock Slide

March 15th 2031, around 6:15 AM: "Hello Dianne," James Coaltonstone said as he stepped from behind the rock slide. "This is just terrible. Horrific. But you look ravishing and I want to let you know I deleted all of the tweets from our early morning spat,"

"Well I feel awful, so don't remind me about that silly twitter thing, can't you see what it really matters. Ninety people are estimated to be dead, twenty men are presumed dead in the mine, and I just fainted in front of the whole planet watching our broadcast.

"I don't think the whole planet is watching your broadcast, I am sure they are waiting for my next tweet," James said.

"You are the most aggravating..." Dianne blurted out.

You are the same old Dianne Black. No one would ever know that you just fainted, and Jackson you need to put on some clothes on before you get frost bitten in places that matter.

"Are we still live?" Dianne asked as she picked herself up from the ground. "Are you saying those things while we are on air?"

"We certainly are and yes I am." James said.

"Is that Mathew I see flyking in all that dust. A boy should not see what I just saw."

"Well that boy appears to be a natural photo journalist," Jackson said.

"That boy is going to be an accountant, just like his mother. It is a much safer job," James interjected.

"So how is Christina?" Dianne asked.

"The same," James said. "She doesn't seem to want to wake up," James explained.

"Which means?" Dianne asked.

"She will be okay. It will take time. We have all been through a lot. This is terrible. I have never seen anything so awful. We might have to leave this as it is because it is all so unstable. That is what the experts from G.O.D are telling me. They are saying that this slide is just huge, really huge. A terrible tragedy to always remember; I am going to build something very special here. That is what I will do," James said.

"So what are you going to do? Start printing out tickets stamped with your brand," Dianne asked.

"Christina, there is no need to be unkind. We will rebuild. There is nothing wrong with the mine, it just needs another entrance. We will have to bring in some track and rebuild the railway. Luckily a young man, I have yet to thank and promote, saved the train from colliding in all this rock and death. It is all so terrible, but at least we managed to save the train, the cargo and 92 passengers and one classified pot that we managed to salvage from Mine Five. The other classified bot seems to be running amok, and if Goodwin were still alive I would blaming him."

"James, whenever you speak I just have more questions. I don't know where to start," Dianne said.

"How about staying focus on this awful rockslide. And think about all the people who have just lost their lives or who were injured," Jackson said. "For once let us think of the victims of all this."

"But those people are just deportees; just illegals," James said.

"Just take one question at a time, and remember here, like in Mina, we work on a ten hour clock and a ten day week." James recommended.

"First question, who were the passengers on your train," Dianne asked.

"Replacements," James replied.

"Replacements? That was fast," Dianne said as she took notes.

"That is not what I meant and why are you taking notes? I did not give you permission to take notes. The Minese were not safe in Pitville even though we are not at war with the Minese people just with the Minese government, like usual the civilians are always the first casualties in these conflicts," James explained.

"Actually we are at war with the Minese. The Minese are mostly here illegally, and are taking jobs from the hard working people of Pitville," Jackson said as both James and Dianne stared at him in disbelief. "I think that is how the Pitville Chapter of G.O.D worded it," Jackson added.

"Anyway, the Minese are now officially deportees, which is a shame. They are better trained and are more experienced in Long Walling than every single one of our local people. My guard bots are networking with my drone watchers and of course my whistle bots. Our boss bots will be performing a supervisory role over the deportees while they remain under our jurisdiction," James explained

"Where will they live?" Dianne asked.

"In the vacant houses that we managed to salvage from the Pitville District housing project, James explained."

"But aren't those buildings occupied?" Dianne asked as she continued writing notes.

"Of course not. How can those houses be occupied while they are being transferred to my new town. Anyway I own those structures. It is up to me to decide when they are vacant," James replied.

"I thought the Pitville Miners dissembled their homes there and reassembled them here, so that they could live and work here," Dianne said, looking troubled.

"Yes, well the Pitville Miners were eligible for these new jobs in Coalton Valley 2, but most of them did not qualify; they did not speak Minese. They may feel those homes are theirs but I actually own them. Many of the minese miners enjoy living in caves and are from the cave district in their homeland. As you know this land is home to many caves which could be fabricated into homes to the best of our ability." James explained.

"I don't understand. The official language spoken on Tut Island is English; Pitville Miners have had experience long walling in Mine Five. How do you justify working with the Minese when we are at war with Mina?" Dianne asked.

"We are not at war with the Minese people, I certainly am not. Our government and their government are at war with each other, I must go, lovely chatting."

"And what about all that anthracite coal that you have been exporting to Mina, a country we are technically at war with?"

"As I said the coal is to help the Minese people and I have nothing against the Minese people," James Coaltonstone said.

"So, dear viewers you heard this straight from the famous King of Coal; James Coaltonstone."

"You, mean this was live?" James asked feeling vulnerable and violated.

"Yes it certainly is."

"How do you justify all this?" Dianne asked.

"Why do you keep making me repeat myself? We are at war with the Minese government not the people, and as I said before, Dianne, my new guard bots function at their best when they speak minese. Dianne we are in the middle of the worst rock slide in Tut Island history, and we should really be discussing these side issues at a later date," James said.

"Just one more question, please. Aren't tut island tax payers who are paying for these roads that your driverless trucks use to transport your coal and what have you to Mina?"

"I suppose so. Dianne look! My Minese are helping to remove the rock.. They just got here and are already helping with the rescue. I think I see some of those awful protestors helping to take rocks away and they have thrown their signs into a pile. Maybe we should set them alight for warmth. I have no idea where our rescue staff are? Some of them were refusing to come here because of the little radiation problem we are rumored to have, as if the waste wasn't in indestructible containers.

"Hold on the phone is ringing, It better be important, It is Mathew.

"Mathew what is wrong?"

"Look out the rubble, can you see a little toddler sitting on the rubble. She is crying her eyes out, can you guys help her?

Dianne, is that a little baby I see on the rubble?" James Coaltonstone asked as he took his binoculars out of his jacket pocket.

Dianne grabbed them from him. "Mathew just phoned us to report that he could see her from the sky,"

"I thought Mathew said that he was flyking to his grandmothers and help her out a bit," James said.

Mathew saw the baby too and decided to take a few photographs

"My God, we have to get to her. She must be terrified. Where are her parents, I wonder?

"Where do you think they might be Di?" Jackson asked then immediately regretted his outburst. "We have to get to her."

"Dianne be careful, I have got her," Jackson said.

"How would you like to come with us, until all this gets sorted out?" Dianne asked.

"The little girl cried hysterically as she called out "Mommy, Daddy".

"Isn't it amazing that all these people are now working together to get people out of the rock slide. The same people who were at each other's throats only a few days ago. Are your parents lost in that rubble?"

The little girl nodded and continued to cry.

"Now for a message from our sponsors," Steve interjected as he stared at his screen oblivious to the growing number of PPZ colleagues who had been crowding into his small office.

THE END

Produced by S.E. McKenzie Productions
First Print Edition September 2016

Enquiries: 1(778)992-2453
Mailing Address:
S. E. McKenzie Productions
168 B 5ᵗʰ St.
Courtenay, BC
V9N 1J4

Email Address:
messidartha@aol.com

http://www.amazon.com/SarahMcKenzie/e/B00H9RWX48/

www.ingramcontent.com/pod-product-compliance
Lightning Source LLC
Chambersburg PA
CBHW070643130626
46555CB00006B/2673